READY to RIDE

Sébastien Pelon

words & pictures

It's a bit dull out there today – the kind of weather
that makes you want to stay inside.

But I'm sooo bored!
I've already done some playing, reading, colouring,
drawing and sticking... I don't know what to do now.

GO AND PLAY OUTSIDE, SWEETHEART,
BUT BE CAREFUL — AND DON'T GO TOO FAR!

The street is empty.

Well, not quite...

I turn round and see a funny shape getting closer.

A ball of fur wearing a pink hat goes past on a tiny bike.

He looks at me.

I hop on my bike and follow him...

... and off we go!

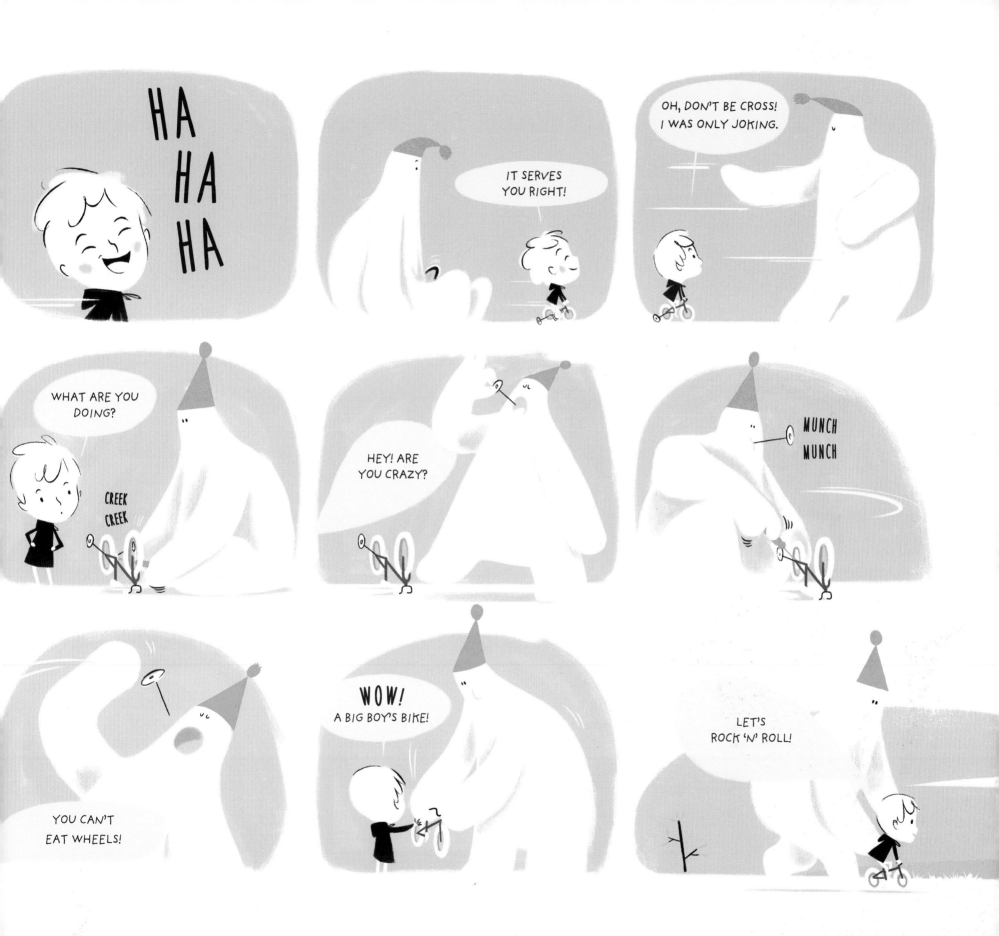

I like feeling the wind on my face.

He stands behind me.

Tall.

Strong.

Friendly.

After all the excitement,
we deserve a little rest.
A ray of sun gently warms us
as the river lulls us to sleep.

Here we go!

Now, I'm riding at the front.

I'm sooo happy.

I go faster...

... except I don't know how to use the brakes yet!

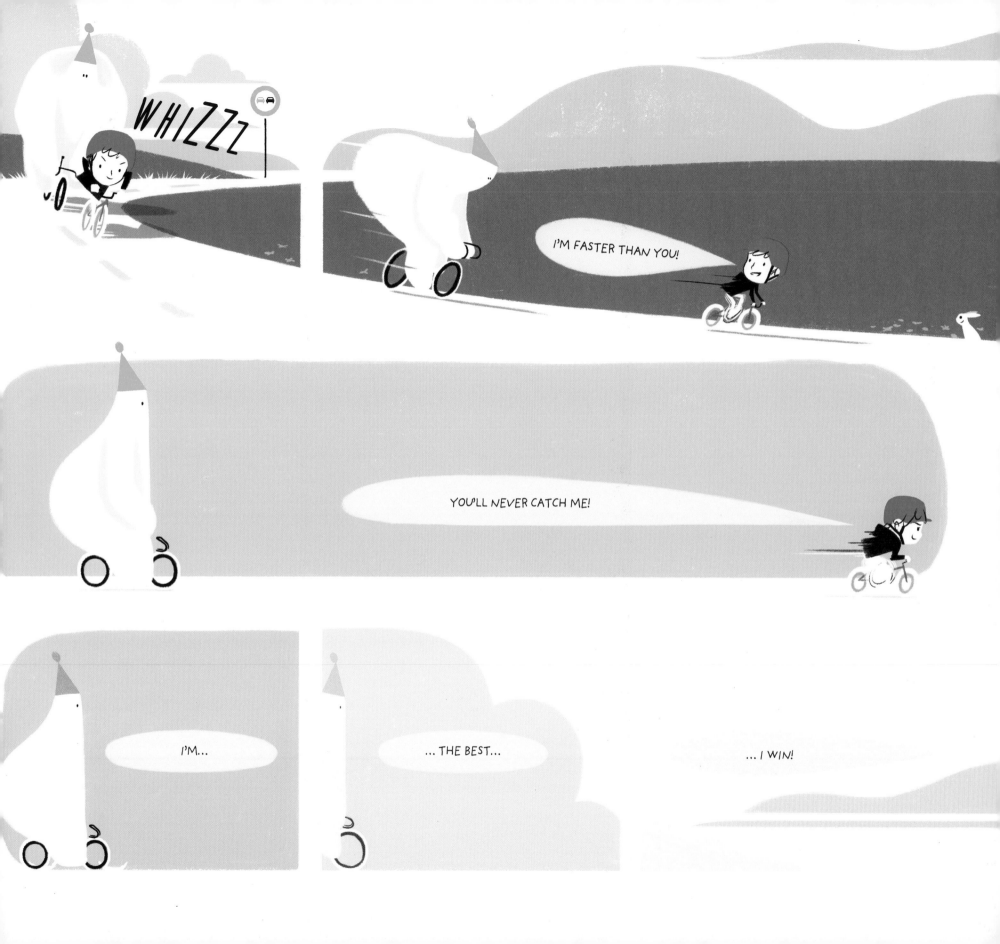

When I turn round,
I'm all by myself - he's gone.
I feel lost.

And a bit scared.
But I look straight ahead
like he showed me.
I know the way.

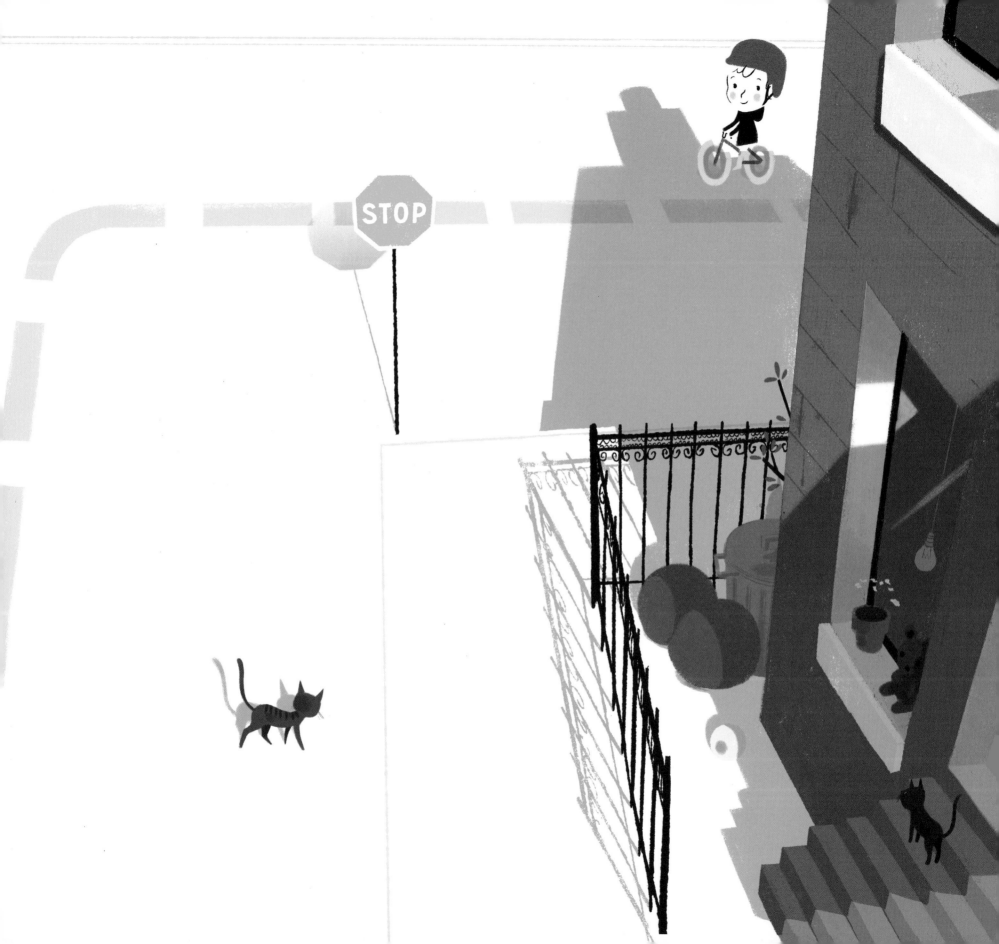

Now the sun is shining.

I take all the time in the world to get home.

I feel a bit sad, but also proud.

I really want to tell Mum and Dad,

but who'll believe that a ball of fur in a pink hat

ate my little wheels?

I put my bike down carefully.

With my helmet on my head and a plaster on my knee,

I feel like a big boy now.

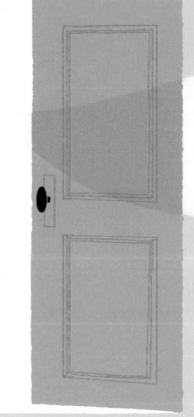

Certificate for a
~ SUPER CYCLIST ~
On ..../............/............,
you took your training wheels off.
You can now ride a bike
like a big boy/girl!

CONGRATULATIONS!